D0236144

Notes for parents

The story has been written in a special way to help young children succeed in their first efforts to read.

Read the whole story aloud first, talking about the pictures as you go. Then encourage your child to read the short, simpler text at the top of each page and read the longer text underneath the pictures yourself. Taking turns with reading builds confidence and children do love joining in.

You can also help your child learn to recognize the important words from this story by looking at the inside back cover where each word is shown next to its picture.

This delightful book provides an enjoyable way for parents and children to share the excitement of learning to read.

Managing designer: **Mary Cartwright** • Photographic manipulation: **John Russell**
Additional models: **Stefan Barnett**, **Les Pickstock**, **Barry Jones**, **Steven Lumley** and **Non Figg**

USBORNE EASY READING

The Runaway Orange

Felicity Brooks

Models by Jo Litchfield ✿ Designed by Non Figg

Language consultant: Dr. Marlynne Grant BSc, CertEd, MEdPsych, PhD, AFBPs, CPsychol

Photography by Howard Allman ✿ Edited by Jenny Tyler

This story is about Polly and Jack Dot.

Here they are with Mr. Dot, Mrs. Dot and Pip the dog.

This is Littletown where they all live.

There is a little blue bird to find on every page

TED SMART

First published in 1999 by Usborne Publishing Ltd. Usborne House, 83-85 Saffron Hill, London EC1N 8RT, England. www.usborne.com Copyright © 1999 Usborne Publishing Ltd. The name Usborne and the device ⊕ are Trade Marks of Usborne Publishing Ltd. All rights reserved. No part of this publication may be reproduced, stored in a retrieval system, or transmitted in any form or by any means electronic, mechanical, photocopying, recording or otherwise, without prior permission of the publisher. UE Printed in Italy.

This edition produced for:
The Book People Ltd, Hall Wood Avenue, Haydock, St Helens WA11 9UL

It's market day in Littletown.

Polly and Jack like the market. Pip likes the market too. It's busy and noisy and there's lots to see.

Mrs. Dot is by the fruit stall.

Oops! She knocks an orange with her bag.
It falls from the stall. Can you see?

The orange rolls away.

Pip thinks it's a big, bouncy ball. He wants to play.
"Come back!" shouts Jack, but Pip doesn't stop.

Mrs. Bird's dogs join the fun.

They jump from her arms. "Come back, Tig!
Come back, Tag!" she cries, but the dogs don't stop.

The dogs chase the runaway orange.

They pass the fish stall.

They pass the cheese stall.

They pass the candy stall...

...and run along the road.

The dogs run into Mr. Bun, the baker.

He nearly drops his tray of cakes.
"Come back!" he shouts. But the dogs don't stop.

Now more dogs join the chase.

A black
dog chases
a big dog...

...who chases
a small dog...

...who chases
a puppy...

...who chases
a spotted dog
who chases...

Stop those dogs!
Stop, Pip, stop!
Woof! Woof!
...Jack who chases...
...Polly who chases...
...Tig and Tag who chase...
...Pip, who chases the runaway orange!

They all run past the café.

There is a CRASH and a BANG, but the dogs don't stop.

They all race down the road.

They pass the butcher's.

They pass the post office.

They pass the bank...

...and pass the pet shop.

A boy kicks the orange.

The dogs stop! They watch the orange fly up in the air. Polly and Jack watch it too.

They chase the orange back up the road.

They pass the bank.

They pass the post office.

They pass the butcher's...

...back to the market!

Pip catches the runaway orange.

He drops it at Mrs. Dot's feet. "Bad dog, Pip," she says. "Look what you've done!"

Littletown is in a mess.

"Oh dear," says Jack. "Oh dear," says Polly.
"Oh dear," says Mrs. Dot.

"Who made this mess?" asks a policeman.

"Well, it all started with a runaway orange..." says Polly. Can *you* remember what happened after that?

The words in *Usborne Easy Reading* books have been carefully chosen and often repeated to help develop your child's early reading skills. Here are some of the important words you will find in *The Runaway Orange:*

Polly

Jack

market

Pip

Mrs. Dot

orange

ball

Mrs. Bird

Mr. Bun

cakes

puppy

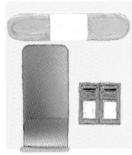

shops

policeman

With thanks to **Eberhard Faber** for providing the **Fimo**® material for models and also to the **Model shop**, 151 City Road, London.